W9-BMW-189

Animal Antics

THE BRAVE BEAR

LUCY COURTENAY

Illustrated by Phil Alderson

SCHOLASTIC INC.

Animals!

Everyone loves animals. Feathery, furry, fierce. Scaly, scary, hairy. Cute, sometimes smelly, and all-around bonkers.

But let's be honest. How well do we really know them?
I know my dog, you might say.
I know my cat and my hamster.

Ah, I say. You may think you know them, but you DON'T.
When you watch them, they do cat-like
and dog-like and hamster-like things.
But what about when you're not watching?
Who knows what they do when you're snoozing
in your bed or when you're at school?

Animal Antics

THE BRAVE BEAR

For Hector, a most excellent swimmer—LC

For Lillah—PA

No part of this publication may be reproduced, stored in a retrieval system, or transmitted in any form or by any means, electronic, mechanical, photocopying, recording, or otherwise, without written permission of the publisher. For information regarding permission, write to Stripes Publishing, an imprint of Magi Publications, 1 The Coda Centre, 189 Munster Road, London SW6 6AW, United Kingdom.

ISBN 978-0-545-47439-9

Text copyright © 2011 by Lucy Courtenay
Illustrations copyright © 2011 by Phil Alderson

All rights reserved. Published by Scholastic Inc., 557 Broadway, New York, NY 10012. SCHOLASTIC and associated logos are trademarks and/or registered trademarks of Scholastic Inc. Lexile is a registered trademark of MetaMetrics, Inc.

12 11 10 9 8 7 6 5 4 3 2 1   12 13 14 15 16 17/0

Printed in the U.S.A.   40

First Scholastic printing, November 2012

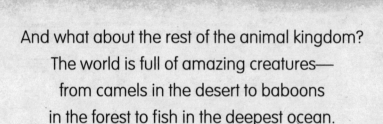

And what about the rest of the animal kingdom?
The world is full of amazing creatures—
from camels in the desert to baboons
in the forest to fish in the deepest ocean.

We know even less about them.
For all we know, they might like dancing. Or doing
handstands. Or having thumb wars. Actually, not thumb
wars, because most animals don't have thumbs.
But you know what I mean.

Maybe we don't know animals as well as we think.
Take POLAR BEARS, for instance. . . .

Chapter One

It was a lovely Arctic morning in Alaska. The freezing wind cut across the landscape, the sky was gray, and the autumn sun was so low on the horizon that it was hardly there at all.

Pongo the polar bear cub waited on the shore as his grandfather swam slowly across Icy Bay toward him. Grandpa's great white paws cut through the water like furry paddles.

He had a large chunk of seal meat in his jaws.

Pongo clapped his paws together. "Well done, Grandpa!" he shouted.

Pongo's grandfather smiled as best he could. It's difficult to smile when you've got half a seal in your mouth.

Pongo was so hungry that he could taste the meat already. "Come on, Grandpa!" he called, hopping from foot to foot. "I'm starving!"

Pongo's grandfather climbed ashore and shook himself dry before putting the meat down. Pongo fell on the food with delight.

"You know, Pongo," Grandpa said as Pongo ate, "you really are old enough to hunt for yourself now. I must try again to teach you to catch seals."

Pongo's food went down the wrong way. He coughed and choked and tried not to remember the last hunting trip he'd been on with Grandpa.

Animal Antics

All the seals had swum out to sea
and laughed at Pongo from
the safety of the water,
because they—and
most of Icy Bay—knew
the terrible truth about
Pongo's Little Problem.

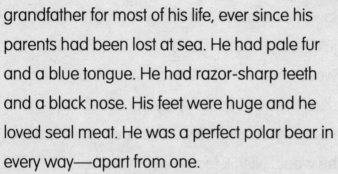

Pongo had lived on
the Arctic shore with his
grandfather for most of his life, ever since his
parents had been lost at sea. He had pale fur
and a blue tongue. He had razor-sharp teeth
and a black nose. His feet were huge and he
loved seal meat. He was a perfect polar bear in
every way—apart from one.

Pongo couldn't swim.

"Oh, please, no!" Pongo gasped aloud. "All
I caught on our last hunting trip was a seagull
and a cold! Do we have to go again?"

"It's time to crack your Little Problem, Pongo," Grandpa said firmly. "Whoever heard of a polar bear that couldn't swim? No, we'll have a swimming lesson right after lunch."

Pongo had been dreading this moment. His grandfather was the strongest swimmer in Icy Bay. He didn't understand the churning feeling in Pongo's tummy whenever the young polar bear thought about swimming. He would laugh if he knew that Pongo's legs turned to jelly every time he got his feet wet. But Grandpa wasn't the one whose parents had been lost at sea. The ocean was scary and dangerous, and Pongo knew as firmly as he knew anything that he would NEVER learn how to swim.

"I don't want a swimming lesson! Can't I catch birds instead of seals?" Pongo said, thinking of the seagull. "And I could eat berries."

His grandfather was looking worried now.

"The last time I saw your parents, I promised to take care of you," he said. "You'll never survive on birds and berries. You need seals. You might be able to catch a few on this shore, but you need to swim in order to reach the best hunting places. Now, come along and let me teach you—"

Pongo backed away. "If you try to give me

a swimming lesson, I'll . . . I'll bite your nose," he said in a trembling voice.

Grandpa blinked. "Tomorrow, then," he said.

"NO!" Pongo shouted.

"But, Pongo—"

Pongo tried desperately to think of something else he could eat. "What about caribou?" he said, in a sudden flash of inspiration. "They're big and meaty and don't live in the ocean. It can't be that hard to catch one—"

"*Excuse* me?"

If polar bears could blush, Pongo would have turned a fiery red. His friend Clara was standing just down the shore, staring at him in horror.

"You would eat a caribou?" Clara repeated. Her antlers quivered on her reindeer head. "I'm

a caribou, Pongo. Does that mean you would
eat *me*?"

"N-no, of course not, Clara. . . ." Pongo stuttered.

"You would eat *me*, even though I'm your
friend?" There were tears in Clara's eyes.
"I may be the only caribou in Icy Bay, but I
thought at least I could count on *you*, Pongo.
You would eat a caribou!" she repeated, as if she
couldn't believe her velvety ears.

Polar bears *can* eat caribou. But luckily for Clara, Pongo was too small, and his grandfather preferred seals.

Grandpa cleared his throat uncomfortably. "Good morning, Clara," he said. "Will you excuse me? Seals to hunt, you know."

He slid back into the water, leaving Pongo and Clara alone.

Clara was still looking upset. Pongo felt awful.

"I really didn't mean that, Clara," he said in a small voice.

Clara's bottom lip was trembling. "Then why did you say it?"

And she stalked away, her large hooves picking carefully across the rocky shore.

Chapter Two

It took half the morning for the caribou to accept Pongo's apology.

"It's all because of my Little Problem, Clara," Pongo confessed when at last Clara started smiling at him again. "Grandpa thinks I'm going to starve if I don't learn how to swim. But you survive okay without swimming, don't you? So why can't I?"

"You're a carnivore, Pongo," said Clara. "You need meat. I'm a herbivore, so moss is fine for me. It's very tasty, actually. Ooh, look! There's a nice patch right there."

Pongo eyed the moss that Clara had started eating. He gave it a sniff. It smelled disgusting. He nibbled off a small piece, and it tasted even worse than it smelled. The thought of eating moss for the rest of his life made Pongo feel even sicker than the thought of going near the water.

Trying to take his mind off the taste of moss between his teeth, Pongo asked, "Do you mind being the only caribou in Icy Bay, Clara?"

"Not at all," said Clara, a little too brightly. "It's great. Just great. I mean it wouldn't be terrible to have a herd. But no, no. It's super. Really."

Pongo wasn't sure he believed her. "I miss my mom and dad," he said, chewing the moss.

"I can still remember their faces. Dad had this long scar down his nose. Mom's tongue was the same pale blue as the summer sky."

"Life goes on, doesn't it, Pongo?" Clara said after a minute. "We just need to make the best of things. And at least you've got your grandfather."

"I guess so," mumbled Pongo.

"Stop eating that moss," Clara said in a bossy voice. "You obviously hate it. Now, fish is meat. Have you thought of fishing from an ice floe? You could lie on the ice and dangle your paw into the water. No swimming needed."

"Great idea!" Pongo said, seizing on the caribou's suggestion. "I'll give it a try right now. Will you help? You know, shout if you can see any fish down in the water?"

"Sure," said Clara. "What are friends for?"

"Not for eating," said Pongo.

"Exactly," said Clara.

There were several ice floes floating close to the shore. If Pongo was careful, he could jump from one to the next without touching the water at all.

With Clara's encouragement, Pongo jumped and landed on his first floe. He scrabbled to grip the ice with his claws, his heart thumping. "Made it," he called. "Can you see any fish?"

"No," Clara called back. "You'll have to try the next one!"

Pongo jumped again and again, trying not to shiver every time the water sloshed beneath him. When he was five ice floes away from the shore, Clara shouted as loudly as she could.

"Yes, Pongo! Down there! To the left! Left a bit more!"

Animal Antics

Pongo squirmed along to the edge on his tummy, dangling his paw into the water. He unsheathed his claws and fished around hopefully. Nothing. He wriggled as close to the edge of the floe as he dared and peered over the side. There were fish down there all right, but they were swimming several yards under the water.

"The fish are too deep for me to catch," he said in dismay.

A wave sloshed at the floe, which pitched to the side and tipped Pongo off. He landed in the deep dark water with a splash. Squealing with terror, he flailed around with his paws. He was sinking. He was drowning—

Suddenly, his grandfather swam up from beneath him, scooping Pongo onto his broad white back.

"I've got you, Pongo. Don't worry, now. Easy does it. Not far to the shore."

Coughing and choking with terror, Pongo clung tightly to his grandfather. He hated the ocean. It had taken his parents away, and now it had tried to drown him, too!

Grandpa climbed ashore at last, and Pongo slid off his back.

Clara galloped over and sniffed Pongo's wet fur in a worried sort of way. "I'm sorry," she said. "I couldn't see how deep the fish were."

"Don't worry, we'll crack your Little Problem soon enough, Pongo," said his grandfather, patting Pongo's back comfortingly.

Pongo lifted his head. "Clara?" he said. "I think I'll give that moss another try. Maybe it's not *so* bad, after all."

Chapter Three

Pongo was determined to prove to Grandpa that he could survive on the sort of food that Clara ate. He lasted two days on a diet of moss and berries before he began to wonder if his own feet might taste nice.

"I've got an idea, Pongo," Grandpa told him on the morning of the third day. "I know a place south of here called Seal Bay. It has plenty of seals at this time of year, all snoozing on the shore. They won't have heard about your Little Problem down there. You're bound to catch one or two of them."

Pongo was so tired and hungry that he nodded in agreement. He ate a few more berries to give him strength and staggered after his grandfather on four shaky white legs.

"Bye!" Clara called, standing beneath a copse of spindly birch trees by the water's edge. "If you see any nice caribous on the way, tell them about me!" she added wistfully. "Not that I *need* another caribou in my life, of course, just . . . tell them, please?"

Pongo and his grandfather walked south along the shore for a few hours. The north wind blew hard at them from behind, ruffling

their fur from tail to nose. Birds soared high in
the sky and sometimes came down to settle
on the scrubby ground. Pongo tried chasing
after a couple, but he couldn't run fast enough.

"Forget the birds, Pongo," said Grandpa,
stopping at last on the top of a snowy ridge.
"Welcome to Seal Bay."

Pongo stared. To the south, the headland
sloped down to the water like a pointed walrus
tusk. As the name of the bay had promised,
the shore was covered with the fat brown

WHOOOSH!

bodies of seals. Large ice floes stretched away from the land for miles, also dotted with seals who hadn't made it as far as the shore. The floes here looked bigger and more solid than the one Pongo had fallen off of. A measly little wave wouldn't make *them* lurch around.

Pongo and Grandpa slid down the snowy ridge on their backs and bottoms as quietly as they could. Pongo's grandfather steered expertly with his paws, and Pongo slid close behind him. As they rolled down to the beach, the seals didn't stir.

"Watch and learn, little bear," whispered Grandpa.

He hurled himself into a pile of seals with a roar of delight.

"Hey!"

"What—"

"A bear! A BEAR!"

Seals started lumbering away in fright— or not lumbering, depending on the speed of Grandpa's teeth. Pongo threw himself into the chaos, grabbing at seals left and right. They were all a little too big for him, but it was fun trying.

Since Grandpa was such an expert hunter, it wasn't long before the two bears were feasting happily.

"Yum," said Grandpa with a belch. "Now let's catch a few more."

Pongo was feeling brave. A full tummy can do that to a bear. "I'll try for the ones out on the ice floes," he said boldly.

Almost jauntily, he jumped onto the nearest ice floe, then the next, and then the next. The seals were still some way off. He took an extra long leap to the biggest floe that he could see before he felt the start of a tummy ache.

I think I'll take a little nap, he thought to himself. *Just till I feel better.*

Pongo settled down and closed his eyes. The floe was very comfortable—it was about ten times bigger than the one he'd fallen off of and it hardly sloshed around at all.

Then he started to dream his favorite dream. He was walking by the water at Icy Bay with his grandfather, feeling warm and happy with a belly full of food. The wind was blowing so hard that the snow on the shore was swirling around like a big cloud. The outlines of two polar bears shimmered in the middle of the snow cloud. As Pongo got closer, the bears grew clearer. They were both smiling at him. One of them had a scar on his nose; the other had a tongue as blue as the sky.

"Mom! Dad! I knew you'd come back! I knew it!"

Pongo opened his eyes, and felt a familiar ache of disappointment. It was just a dream.

He rolled over and yawned. Then he blinked. He blinked again. Where was he? Where were all the other ice floes? Where was the shore—and where was his grandfather?

Animal Antics

"Grandpa?" he called, feeling alarmed.

Pongo stared at the wide gray sea that surrounded him. His ice floe was sailing silently through the waves like a lonely, craggy white boat. The shore was nowhere to be seen.

Chapter Four

Pongo panicked. He started running up and down the big ice floe.

"Grandpa! Clara! Someone help me!"

His voice bounced across the water. There was no answer.

Pongo tried to think. How long had he been asleep? How far away was the shore? He hadn't napped for *that* long. Had he?

"Grandpa!" he called again forlornly.

The floe was caught in the ocean current and moving quite fast. Pongo stared at the water slipping by. The bitter wind smoothed his fur from nose to tail. *The north wind,* he thought. He was facing north, and sailing south.

Is this what happened to my parents? he wondered. *Did they float south on an ice floe, too?* He shivered.

For the first time in his life, he wished he could swim.

Pongo lost track of time. He lay down at the back of the floe and gazed north. A large piece of ice broke off from right under his nose, making Pongo howl in fright. It was getting warmer—the little polar bear could feel it. His ice floe was melting.

Animal Antics

More time passed. What little sun there
was started to creep toward the horizon.
Pongo tried to keep his spirits up by singing
a song about fish that a bald eagle friend of
Grandpa's had once taught him.

SLICKHEAD, PRICKLEBACK,
BURBOT, AND STICKLEBACK,
HAKE, COD, HALIBUT, AND DAGGERFISH, TOO!
OH HOW I'D LOVE TO MUNCH,
GOBBLE, CHOMP, AND CHASE AND CRUNCH
ALL THE FISH I'D EVER WISH UNTIL
I'M THROUGH.

Pongo sang it over and over, halibut and daggerfish swimming endlessly through his brain. Another bit of the ice floe broke away and sailed off. It was getting too small for comfort. Pongo swallowed hard and started singing again.

Eventually, he fell asleep because there wasn't anything else to do. This time his dreams were full of deep water, and he woke up feeling more scared than ever.

And then—wonderfully, amazingly—a thin strip of land appeared on the late afternoon horizon. Pongo felt his tummy leap with hope. The land got closer as the current swept him toward it.

At last, the ice floe bumped gently against a spit of rock. Pongo managed to scramble ashore just as the ice fell to pieces.

Gulping with relief, the young polar bear

saw that he was standing on the edge of a sweeping green bay. Tall trees towered all around him, standing a little way back from the sandy shore. There was a warm smell of pine needles and moss and living things. Pongo could have done without the smell of moss, but he was alive! He was safe! He was dry!

There was only one problem.

He had absolutely no idea where he was.

"Hello?" he called. There was no reply.

He trotted up the beach and into the trees, looking around. Strange birds twittered among the branches and Pongo could hear small animals creeping around in the undergrowth. A lone crow circled overhead.

Pongo stopped when he reached the far side of the woods. A sparkling river tumbled past him, shining and glinting in the sinking sun. Two grizzly bears were standing at the top of some rapids up ahead. They hadn't seen Pongo.

"Here they come, George," said the bigger of the two bears. She licked her lips.

"I can see them, Mom!" said George in excitement. "I can see the salmon!"

There was a flash of silver, and a fish leaped out of the water before plunging back in again. The crow sank lower, watching the fish as carefully as the bears were.

The fish hurled themselves closer to the rapids. They were working hard to swim upstream, and weren't getting very far. Then the fish at the front made a mighty leap—and the big bear caught it in one outstretched paw. The little bear clapped.

"Well done, Mom!"

"You take the next one, son," said the big bear.

Silver salmon cascaded up the river, straight into the grizzly bears' waiting paws. The crow was waiting nearby, ready to land and eat the leftovers lying on the shore.

Pongo was a polite bear, so he waited for the grizzly bears to finish eating. As they washed their paws in the river and started cleaning their fur, he came out of the shadows.

"Um, excuse me?" he said. "I'm lost and I was wondering—"

The bears' eyes widened as they took in the young white cub trotting toward them. The crow shot straight up into the air again in a whirl of black feathers.

"Mom!" wailed the little one. "What's that?"

"Run, George!" yelped the big bear in terror. "It's a GHOST BEAR!"

Chapter Five

"Wait!" shouted Pongo.

It was too late. The grizzly bears had both run far into the darkness of the pine woods.

"Ghost bear!" croaked the crow. It turned, heading back toward the shore. "Ghost bear! Ghost bear!" And then the crow was gone, too.

How can anyone think I'm a ghost? Pongo wondered. It was almost funny. He stared at his reflection in the river. It was true that he was white, and ghosts were white. Perhaps they'd never seen a polar bear before.

He wished the bears hadn't run off. He wished the crow hadn't flown away. He needed to ask someone where he was, and how he could get home again.

Feeling lonely and lost, Pongo sat down on the bank of the river and started to cry.

We just need to make the best of things, he heard Clara saying in his head. *And at least you've got your grandfather.*

He had to get back to Grandpa! He couldn't give up now. Pongo wiped his nose and stood up. He padded back through the trees, determined to find someone he could ask about finding his way home.

"Ghost bear!" cawed the crow overhead as Pongo emerged on the shore again, his pale fur shining in the setting sun. "Run for your lives!"

A wave of birds and animals rushed away from the water's edge and into the trees. Worried voices reached Pongo's ears from within the forest.

"White! Pure white!"

"Cranley the crow says it's already scared Gloria and George off the salmon waterfall."

"It's got big, evil teeth."

"Red eyes, too."

"Mommy, I don't want to see a ghost bear!"

I'M NOT A GHOST!

Pongo's voice echoed back at him,
bouncing off the silent trees.

He was all alone.

For the next two days, Pongo padded around
the empty woods, hoping to find someone to
talk to. But it was as if all the creatures of Pine
Tree Bay had disappeared into thin air. It had
been a long time now since Pongo had feasted
on Grandpa's seals, and he was starving.

On the morning of the third day, Pongo
saw a large bald eagle swoop down from
the sky, heading for the river with its talons
outstretched. Its claws splashed into the water
and pulled out a fat and shining fish. Then with
two or three powerful wingbeats, it flew to the
riverbank and dropped its catch on the ground.

Pongo was so hungry that he didn't stop

to think. He bolted out of the woods and jumped on the salmon. The eagle flapped back in surprise.

"Hey!"

"Sorry," Pongo mumbled, his mouth full of fish. "Had to eat."

The eagle's eyes flashed. "Don't you know it's rude to steal someone else's food?"

Pongo had already eaten most of the salmon. He felt a hundred times better. "I know," he said guiltily. "I'm really very grateful. Do you mind catching another one?"

"I have half a mind to peck you very hard," the eagle said.

Pongo looked at its sharp beak and gulped. "Sorry," he said again.

"You're the one they call the ghost bear, I suppose?" the eagle said. "Never seen a ghost with an appetite before."

"I'm not a ghost," Pongo said, upset. "But I wish I was. Then I wouldn't get so hungry."

"The creatures around here are all as brainless as barnacles," said the eagle, looking Pongo over with its fierce yellow eyes. "Why, you're just a baby polar bear! Big evil teeth and red eyes indeed. That Cranley has a big beak. Since you've eaten my fish, youngster, I might as well know your name."

"Pongo," said Pongo, feeling grateful that the eagle was being kind to him. It felt like forever since he'd had a conversation.

"What's yours?"

"Eddie." The eagle gazed thoughtfully at him. "I know an old polar bear farther north who looks a bit like you. Think you might be related?"

Pongo stared. "You're not the eagle who once taught me a song, are you?"

The eagle's eyes glinted.

"It *is* you!" Pongo said happily.

The eagle smiled. "You've grown up since I last saw you. What are you doing so far south?"

Pongo explained what had happened, adding, "I want to go home, but I don't know how to get there. Is it far?"

"It's tricky by land," said Eddie thoughtfully. "The shore wriggles up and down like an eel, and the terrain is tough going for all but the strongest caribou. But it's not difficult if you can fly or swim, stopping off at the headlands as you go. Good thing you're a polar bear, eh?"

He looked at Pongo, clearly expecting the little bear to smile with relief.

"I can't swim," said Pongo quietly.

Eddie looked amazed. "But surely your grandfather taught you?"

"My parents swam off one day and never

came back," said Pongo, even more quietly. "I don't like the ocean very much."

"I'm very sorry to hear it," said Eddie. "But that doesn't stop *you* from swimming, does it?"

"Yes," said Pongo, in the quietest voice of all. "I'm afraid it does."

Eddie thought for a moment. "We'll just have to figure something out, won't we?" he said. "Your grandfather will be missing you, and I can't have you eating my fish forevermore. Meet me on the shore this afternoon. There's someone I'd like you to meet."

Chapter Six

The eagle met Pongo on the shore as planned.

"I hope you caught another fish," said Pongo. He was still feeling guilty about stealing Eddie's breakfast.

"Of course I did," said Eddie. "I'm not known as the world's most marvelous fish catcher for nothing. Now, where is Bert when you need him?"

The eagle took off and swept low over the water in the bay. He circled around for a moment before plunging down to the sea.

"Bert!" Pongo heard him call as he flapped up into the air again. "Bring your head above water—there you go."

A large white dolphin-like creature breached the surface and blinked up at Eddie. "Oh, it's you, Eddie," it said in a high, twittering sort of voice.

"Come and meet a friend of mine," said Eddie. "Can you swim closer to the shore?"

"Closer to the shore?" Bert twittered. "Don't you know what happens when we get too close to the shore? We get stuck like—well, beached whales. I'd never hear the end of it from my family."

"Just a little closer," Eddie coaxed.

Bert grumbled but swam a little nearer to the land.

Animal Antics

"Pongo, meet Bert the beluga whale," said Eddie, landing on the shore. "Bert, meet Pongo the polar bear—your new swimming student."

"Hello," said Pongo nervously.

Bert coughed out a shocked spout of water. "I can't give him swimming lessons!" he squeaked in horror.

"Yes, you can," said Eddie. "If we don't teach Pongo how to swim, he'll never get home and he'll keep stealing my fish. So I'll be too hungry to fly around looking for food for *you* as

well as me. Besides, I know his grandfather."

"But he's a polar bear, Eddie!" said the beluga whale. "Polar bears eat belugas!"

"We do?" said Pongo, surprised. Bert the beluga looked much too big to eat.

"Come on, Bert," said Eddie. "As a favor to me. I show you all the best crab spots, don't I? The finest shrimping coves? He's just a baby and you're his only chance. You've got a kind heart under all that blubber. Teach this youngster to swim."

"Hmph," said Bert. He looked at Pongo.
"Do you want to learn how to swim, bear?"

"No," said Pongo truthfully. His knees felt
shaky at the thought. "But I have to or I'll never
get home." He tried to smile in a harmless,
untoothy sort of way.

"Give me your word that this grandfather of
yours won't eat me, and that's one less polar
bear I have to worry about," said Bert at last.

"He won't," Pongo promised.

"That's decided, then," said Eddie with a
nod. "I'll leave you in Bert's capable flippers,
Pongo. And Bert? Remind me later to tell
you about the fat cluster of lobsters I spotted
yesterday afternoon."

Eddie rose into the air and flew away over
the dark tops of the pine trees.

"Did I just agree to teach a polar bear to
swim?" Bert muttered. "I must be crazy."

Animal Antics

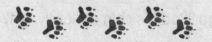

The lesson started badly. Pongo panicked every time his tummy got wet, and he blundered out of the water.

"This is like trying to teach an octopus to stand on its head!" the beluga twittered from the deeper part of the bay as Pongo thrashed around in the water, making for the shore. "Hopeless! What's the matter with you?"

SPLASH!

Pongo lifted his chin defiantly. "My parents went hunting together and drowned when I was a baby, okay? So I have a little trouble with water."

Bert frowned. "When was this?"

"Last year. At least, I think they drowned. They never came back."

"Hunting *together*, you say?" Bert whistled. "Two adults hunting together is unusual. I saw two bears hunting together just the other day—one male, one female."

Pongo's heart jumped in his chest. "You did?"

"Believe me, it's a sight no beluga is likely to forget," Bert said with feeling. "I was looking for shrimp along the Russian shore. That's across from Alaska, you know."

Pongo knew it was a crazy question. He was sure his parents were dead. But he asked it anyway. "Did the male bear have a long scar across his nose?"

"Yes," said Bert. "I believe he did."

Pongo tried to stay calm. Lots of polar bears had scarred noses.

"Did . . . did you notice anything unusual about the female bear?"

Bert shivered. "She saw me and licked her lips, and I was out of there quicker than a daggerfish. That tongue was as blue as the summer sky. Paler than any bear's I've ever seen. Gives me chills just thinking about it."

"And they were alive?" Pongo asked joyfully. "They weren't drowned?"

"Very much alive, I'm afraid," said Bert. "No offense."

Chapter seven

If Bert hadn't been in deep water, Pongo would have jumped in and hugged him and kissed him on the tip of his white nose.

"My parents didn't drown," he repeated in wonder. "They're still alive and they didn't drown!"

Pongo walked into the water. Up to his knees. Up to his tummy. Right up to his chin.

"Good!" said Bert. "Well done! Now . . ."

Pongo closed his eyes and thought about his parents, standing on a dry brown Russian beach. He could do this. It wasn't that scary.

Slowly, he lifted his feet and started to paddle.

"I thought Eddie said you needed lessons!" twittered Bert in surprise as Pongo swam around in a slow, careful circle, not too far from the shore. "One minute you're a scaredy bear, the next minute you're not!"

Animal Antics

The polar bear cub scrambled ashore
and shook his fur dry. He took a deep breath,
feeling his body tingling all over. "It must be
your teaching, Bert." He grinned. "Should I try it
again?"

Pongo couldn't remember a happier
afternoon than the one he spent with Bert
the beluga whale. He started swimming
deeper with each circle
he made. It was easy
once he got the hang
of it. As he got braver
he tried a roll, and
then a dive. And
the whole time,
Pongo was
thinking,

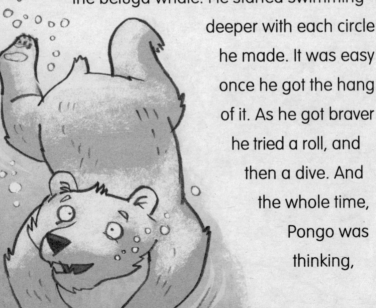

My parents are alive! They're okay!

"There!" Eddie cried in triumph, appearing in the sky as Pongo paddled around Bert for the eighth time. "I knew you could do it with the right teacher, Pongo!"

"Easiest lobsters I ever earned," squeaked Bert as Pongo waded out of the water for a good shake. "And on the subject of lobsters . . . ?"

"Two bays north of here, tucked into a little creek," Eddie said, landing on the shore. "Hard for the average eyes to spot," he added, "but of course I am an eagle, so I saw them right away."

Bert gave Eddie a blast of thanks from his blowhole.

"Well, Pongo," he said, turning back to the little bear. "You don't need me anymore. Just keep practicing and you'll be ready to swim home in no time at all." And he sank from view.

"Thanks, Bert!" Pongo shouted, galloping up the shore after the beluga's bubble trail. "I'll tell my grandpa AND my parents not to eat you! So that's FOUR polar bears you don't have to worry about because when I'm grown up I won't eat you, either!"

When the beluga had gone, Pongo trotted back to Eddie.

"Mom and Dad are okay, Eddie!" he said. "Bert saw them. They're alive!"

Eddie looked surprised. "Are you sure it was them?"

"Bert described them perfectly," said Pongo happily.

"I don't want to spoil things," said Eddie, "but if they're still alive, why have they never come home?"

Pongo frowned. "I don't know," he said.

Eddie stretched out his wings. "I hope that they are alive, Pongo," he said. "But try not to get your hopes up. See you later."

Pongo watched the eagle launch himself into the sky, then hurtle down toward the water like a great black arrow.

Why didn't *my parents come home?* Pongo wondered as Eddie pulled back into the sky again with a fish in his claws. It did seem a little weird, now that he thought about it. He had to find out more.

Animal Antics

Diving off the rocks, he started swimming after the beluga whale. "Bert!" he shouted. "I've got more questions about my parents! BERT!"

The lobsters Bert wanted were two bays north, Eddie had said. Pongo concentrated on swimming slowly and carefully. He wasn't afraid, but he was aware that he was still young and might tire himself out. He paddled to the shore three or four times to rest.

Two bays north was a small cove that looked like a sea monster had taken a bite out of the coastline. Pongo saw Bert at once, up near the shore.

"Bert!" he shouted, paddling toward the beluga. To his surprise, his feet touched the bottom more quickly than he had been expecting. He splashed and waded on. "Bert, it's me. I just wanted to ask you . . ."

He stopped. He could see more of Bert's big body in the shallow water than he was expecting.

"Oh, no!" he said in horror.

"Never thought . . . I'd be pleased . . . to see a polar . . . bear," Bert twittered, panting heavily. "Lobsters . . . were too shallow. I'm . . . stuck. Help me, Pongo. . . . Got to . . . get back in the water . . . or I'll . . . die."

Chapter Eight

Pongo didn't know what to do. He was too small to push Bert back into the deeper water on his own.

The beluga was having trouble breathing. His heavy body, which normally floated in the water like a big white feather, was now crushing his lungs.

"Help . . ." he panted again.

"It'll be okay, Bert," Pongo said desperately. "I'll get you out of this."

"Ghost bear!" someone shouted from the shore. "Cranley the crow said there was a ghost bear in Pine Tree Bay—"

"I'M NOT A GHOST!" Pongo shouted back, trying to see who was speaking. "I'm a polar bear! Please, this beluga needs help!"

A pair of dark brown beavers peeped over the top of a sturdy dam of sticks higher up the shore. The male beaver patted his wife's paw.

"Leave this to me, Beryl. I've heard of polar bears." He cleared his throat. "HOW CAN WE HELP?" he said loudly, as if Pongo spoke a different language.

"I don't know," said poor Pongo. "I wish I did."

"Those darn . . . lobsters . . ." squeaked the beluga weakly.

The male beaver trotted down to the water, followed by his wife. "Hmm," he said, frowning at Bert. "You need more water or you'll never push him back. But high tide's not for another few hours. Sorry not to be of more help."

Suddenly, Pongo had an idea. "Your dam," he said, looking up at the big wooden construction. "Do you need it?"

The male beaver looked shocked. "Of course we need it. We're beavers. It's our home!"

"Could you take it down temporarily?" Pongo asked hopefully. "There must be lots of water behind it. If the dam wasn't there, the river would wash down and lift my friend off the shore."

Animal Antics

The male beaver looked even more shocked. "Do you have any idea how long that dam took to build?"

"Can't breathe . . ." whispered Bert.

"Do as the bear says, Boris."

A caribou was standing under the trees. For a crazy minute, Pongo thought Clara had appeared on the shore. But this caribou was too big to be Clara.

The newcomer trotted over to the dam. "Come on, Boris," he said. "Your wife loves building dams. If we knock this one down, she can start all over again."

The female beaver looked excited. "Ooh! Can we, Boris?"

"But it took so long!" Boris cried.

"Please," Pongo begged.

"Well, I suppose so," said Boris reluctantly. "But how do we get it down quickly?"

"Leave that to me," said the big caribou.

He splashed into the water behind the dam and charged at the structure with his antlers down. There was a mighty CRASH.

Branches and twigs exploded into the air—and
a flood of water rushed down the sloping shore.

"Yippee!" shouted Beryl the beaver. Her
husband put his face in his paws.

"NOW, Bert!" Pongo shouted, struggling to
stay on his feet in the whoosh of water pouring
into the sea. "Swim!"

Bert flicked his tail feebly. Pongo put all his
strength into pushing Bert off the pebbles. And
suddenly the beluga lifted free.

CRASH!

Panting, Pongo collapsed on the shore as Bert sank into the deeper water. Beryl the beaver cheered and kissed her husband. The big caribou tossed a large bunch of twigs off his velvet antlers and shook his wet body.

"I swear I'll never be rude about polar bears again!" Bert squealed, whistling and clicking like crazy as he rose to the surface. "Thank you, Pongo! Mr. and Mrs. Beaver, what can I say? And you, too, Mr. Caribou!"

"Please, Bert!" Pongo called before the delighted beluga could swim away. "I wanted to ask you something else about my—about the bears you saw!"

"Ask anything you like," shouted Bert. "Except for a bite out of my tail."

"If those bears *were* my parents—why do you think they haven't come home to me and Grandpa?" Pongo said, a little breathlessly.

"Wouldn't you go home to your cub if you could? I just wondered . . ."

"What was stopping them?" said Bert. "They were stranded, I would say. The sea was open from Russia to Alaska, you see. Too far for polar bears to swim. The pack ice they'd traveled on had probably melted away. No pack ice means no way home."

Chapter Nine

Eddie flew into sight as Pongo lay on the shore
and got his breath back. Bert had swum out
of the bay already, heading for the deepest
water he could find.

"Hey there, little bear!" the eagle called.
"Heading home without saying good-bye?"

He landed beside Pongo, and the young
polar bear told him about Bert's narrow escape.

"And it was thanks to the beavers and this kind caribou," Pongo finished, looking shyly at the big caribou still standing under the trees.

"Good for you, Charles," Eddie said to the caribou. "Pongo, meet Charles, lone caribou of the pine woods. And Charles, meet Pongo, a polar bear who's a long way from home."

Charles the caribou nodded politely at Pongo.

"You were amazing," Pongo said.

"Was I?" said Charles, looking pleased.

Pongo shook himself dry. "Bert said my parents looked like they were stuck," he told Eddie. "There hasn't been ice between Alaska and Russia this year, and not even my grandfather could swim the whole way without any ice to rest on every now and then."

"Maybe there will be ice this winter," Eddie said.

"Maybe," said Pongo. "I hope so."

"It's better than thinking they're dead, isn't it?" Eddie asked kindly.

Pongo thought that it was, but he still felt sad about it. He reminded himself how lucky he was to have Grandpa. And with luck, it wouldn't be long now until he saw Grandpa again.

Then he remembered something that put the thought of his parents out of his mind. "Did Eddie say you were a lone caribou, Charles?" he asked the big caribou, who was still standing under the trees.

"Sadly, yes," said Charles. He cleared his throat. "But I don't mind. Not really. Not too much. Not usually."

Pongo thought he sounded just like Clara. He remembered Clara's last words to him just before he and Grandpa left on their fishing trip:

If you see any nice caribous on the way, tell them about me!

"Would you be interested in a trip up north, Charles?" Pongo asked. "There's a caribou I think you should meet. She's alone, just like you."

Charles's eyes widened. He looked excited.

"What a good idea!" said Eddie. "I'd like to go on another trip in that direction myself."

"Well," said Pongo on impulse. "We're already two coves in the right direction. Why don't we all go north? Right now?"

Animal Antics

Animals don't need to pack their suitcases
or find their passports. As soon as Eddie
and Charles agreed to come with him,
Pongo plunged into the water. He and Eddie
arranged to meet Charles in the next cove, just
as soon as the caribou could make it across
the mountainous coast.

Eddie flew high overhead, sometimes
dipping down to warn Pongo about a tricky
current that he'd spotted with his eagle eyes,
or to direct him to the next piece of land where
Pongo could get his breath back
and they could meet
Charles. Since there
were no seals, Eddie
caught plenty
of fish, which
he shared with
Pongo. The little

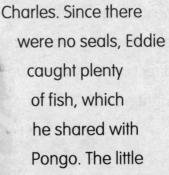

bear thought that
having wings
might be the most
useful thing in the
world.

The coast grew
snowier as they got farther north. Icy
mountains appeared in the distance, and gray
clouds began rolling in. Pongo smelled the air
happily. It was getting colder.

When they met ashore for the tenth time,
Pongo noticed that the local animals had
stopped calling him "ghost bear."

"They're probably used to polar bears
around here," Charles said. "We're much
farther north now." He looked hopefully into
the trees. "Is, um, your friend near here, do
you know?"

"She won't be far," Pongo promised.

The shape of the coast was starting to look familiar. Pongo swam and paddled, jumped across ice floes and rested ashore, then swam and paddled some more. Eddie circled lazily overhead while Charles trotted up and down the mountainous coast as fast as his big feet would let him, checking every time they met along the shore: "Are we almost there?"

Grandpa will be amazed to see me swimming, Pongo thought, paddling around the pointed, tusk-like headland that marked the edge of Seal Bay. In fact, his grandfather would probably be amazed to see him at all. And wait till he heard the news about Pongo's parents!

"Oh, yes," screeched Eddie overhead. "Fish heaven!"

GULP!

As the bald eagle dived into the sea, Pongo scrambled onto one of Seal Bay's ice floes. He jumped, zigzagging his way from floe to floe until his toes touched down on the shore.

Charles was already waiting, standing on a seal-free stretch of the icy beach. Only it wasn't Charles at all.

"PONGO!" shouted Clara with delight. "Pongo, it's you! *It's you, it's you, it's you!*"

Chapter Ten

Words poured out of Clara like the water from the beavers' dam.

"You're alive! Your grandfather has been beside himself! 'I shouldn't have taken him to Seal Bay,' he said! 'I should have taken care of Pongo just as I promised his parents,' he said! He almost lost his fur with grief. And so did I. We've been camped out here ever since you left, hoping you'd return. I haven't eaten a mouthful of moss for *days*. And look at you! So big! So *fierce*! I swear you've grown!"

"Grrrr," said Pongo, putting up his paws in a pretend-fierce way and laughing at his friend's happy face.

"No caribou-eating, please," said Clara with a giggle.

Eddie landed a short distance from Clara, making the caribou jump.

"Goodness, what a large bird," she said. "Have we met?"

Pongo introduced Clara to Eddie. He glanced behind Clara in case Charles had appeared. There was no sign of the big caribou yet. He hoped Charles hadn't gotten lost.

"But where have you *been*?" Clara demanded.

"I sailed south on an ice floe by mistake."

Pongo grinned. "And then I swam home again."

Clara blinked. "You *swam*?"

"Yes," Pongo said proudly. "I learned how to do it and it's easy. And listen to this. I think my parents are alive, Clara!"

Clara's eyes widened. "Alive?"

"It sounds like they're stuck on the Russian coast at the moment," Pongo rushed on, "but as soon as there's some ice between Russia and Alaska, they'll hopefully come home. Isn't that fantastic?"

"Really fantastic, Pongo," Clara replied with a weak smile and a shaky voice. "I'm so happy for you!" Two big fat tears appeared in her wide brown eyes. She hung her head. The tears rolled off her nose and froze on the ground like diamonds. Pongo suddenly felt really bad. His parents were alive and maybe coming back one day soon. But Clara was still by herself.

Just then, Charles appeared over the ridge, puffing and panting and shaking snow off his hooves.

"Clara, it's okay," Pongo said, his heart lifting again. "You don't have to be on your own anymore. I've brought someone to meet you."

Clara looked up and spotted Charles. She looked thunderstruck. Charles stopped shaking snow off his hooves and looked thunderstruck, too.

Animal Antics

"H-hello," Charles stammered at last. "You have beautiful antlers."

"And you have very nice hooves," Clara said. She sounded a little dazed.

"I love a happy ending!" cried Eddie, circling high in the gray Arctic sky.

"Pongo!"

Pongo's grandfather came lumbering over the ridge, slipping and sliding on his big white furry bottom. "Pongo!" he shouted again.

"Grandpa!"

Pongo raced toward Grandpa, who swept him into a big bear hug. "You'll never guess where I've been, Grandpa! Do you remember Eddie? Oh—and I've got the most amazing news!"

Cranley the crow soared on the wind, enjoying the breeze under his long black wings. He'd come farther north than usual. Spying a strip of brown land beneath him, he fluttered down to rest and preen his feathers.

He got the fright of his life as two huge white bears loomed ahead of him on the big brown rocks.

"The ice is coming," said the larger one.

"Of course it is, my love," said the other. "We'll see little Pongo very soon."

"*Two* ghost bears!" Cranley squawked in horror. "*Two very BIG ghost bears!*"

And a little more...

Two years later, Bert the beluga whale was swimming through the dark blue water off the Alaskan coast with his family.

"How many times have we told you about getting too close to the shore, Bert?" said his mom.

"You know what happened last time," his sister reminded him.

"Beaching yourself just for a bunch of lobsters!" sighed his aunt.

"Give it a rest, you guys!" Bert shouted.

The family swam to the surface for air, with
Bert's mother, sister, and aunt still going on
about the lobsters.

"Whoops," squeaked Bert, as they came
face-to-face with the biggest polar bear
they'd ever seen.

"Bert?" said the huge bear.

Bert stared. *"Pongo?"*

Pongo grinned at him. "Go back into the water now," he said, waving a full-grown paw the size of Bert's head. "And take your family with you. I keep my promises."

"You . . . you know that bear?" twittered Bert's mother faintly as the belugas sank under the water again.

"Yes," Bert said. "And I'll have him go after you if you ever mention those lobsters again."

THE END

Totally True

Beluga whales are also known as sea canaries because of their twittering voices.

Polar bear fur is hollow. Reflected light makes it look white.

When they are ready to spawn, salmon swim upriver to the exact place they hatched.

"Arctic" comes from the Greek word for *bear*.

Climate change is melting the ice that polar bears depend on.

Caribou are called reindeer in Europe.

**Also
Available:**

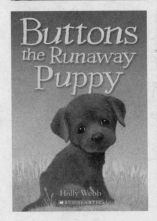

Sam the Stolen Puppy

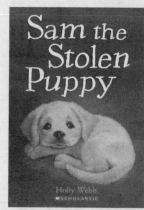

Holly Webb
SCHOLASTIC

Alfie all Alone

Holly Webb
SCHOLASTIC

From the author of LOST IN THE SNOW
Max the Missing Puppy

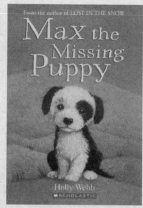

Holly Webb
SCHOLASTIC

Timmy in Trouble

Holly Webb
SCHOLASTIC

Ellie the Homesick Puppy

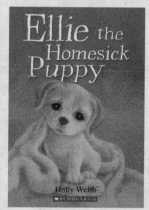

Holly Webb
SCHOLASTIC

Jess the Lonely Puppy

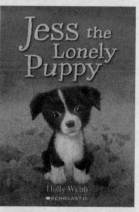

Holly Webb
SCHOLASTIC

Misty the Abandoned Kitten

Holly Webb
SCHOLASTIC

Lucky the Rescued Puppy

Holly Webb
SCHOLASTIC

Whiskers the Lonely Kitten

Holly Webb
SCHOLASTIC

Don't miss . . .

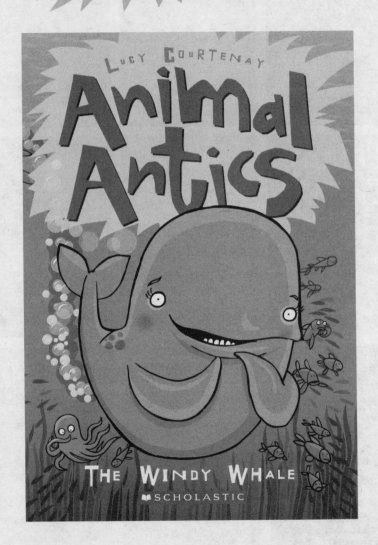

LUCY COURTENAY

Animal Antics

THE WINDY WHALE

SCHOLASTIC